Mini Sagas From The West Midlands

Edited By Sarah Washer

First published in Great Britain in 2018 by:

 Young**Writers**

Young Writers
Remus House
Coltsfoot Drive
Peterborough
PE2 9BF
Telephone: 01733 890066
Website: www.youngwriters.co.uk

FOREWORD

Young Writers was created in 1991 with the express purpose of promoting and encouraging creative writing. Each competition we create is tailored to the relevant age group, hopefully giving each child the inspiration and incentive to create their own piece of work, whether it's a poem or a short story. We truly believe that seeing their work in print gives pupils a sense of achievement and pride in their work and themselves.

Every day children bring their toys to life, creating fantastic worlds and exciting adventures, using nothing more than the power of their imagination. What better subject then for primary school pupils to write about, capturing these ideas in a mini saga – a story of just 100 words. With so few words to work with, these young writers have really had to consider their words carefully, honing their writing skills so that every word counts towards creating a complete story.

Within these pages you will find stories about toys coming to life when we're not looking and tales of peril when toys go missing or get lost! Some young writers went even further into the idea of play and imagination, and you may find magical lands or fantastic adventures as they explore their creativity. Each one showcases the talent of these budding new writers as they learn the skills of writing, and we hope you are as entertained by them as we are.

CONTENTS

King Henry VIII Preparatory School, Coventry

James Wade (11)	58
Akanksha Linesh (10)	59
Haresh Raguram (9)	60
Amba Bodali-Bosson (8)	61
Oliver Wang (10)	62
Arjun Vadgama (8)	63
Silvia Iuga (10)	64
Himmat Singh Chana (10)	65
Sukhmani Kaur (10)	66
William He (9)	67
Xanthe Wong (7)	68
Eloise Mills (11)	69
Aman Marwaha (7)	70
Raveena Dave	71
Aanya Kachhala (10)	72
Sian Madahar (8)	73
Kiran Heer (9)	74
Mara Iuga (11)	75
Atharva Karn (9)	76
Lucy Wade (9)	77
Anastasia O'Neill (9)	78
Gabriella Olivia Duggan (9)	79
Hannah Alijan Kazmi (9)	80
Alexa Duggan (8)	81

Lote Tree Primary School, Foleshill

Amirah Thompson (10)	82
Maryam Haroon (10)	83
Fahmida Begum (10)	84
Isa Khaleel (10)	85
Safiya Snaaullah (10)	86
Ismaeel Yousuf (10)	87

Moat Farm Junior School, Oldbury

Tonisha Malhi (11)	88
Vina Hassan (10)	89
Remarn Taylor (10)	90

Aeshveer Maan	91
Willow Harmony Moore (9)	92
Faith Abigail Green (9)	93
Sumayyah Aliyah Mahmood (11)	94
Rayiah Hussain (10)	95
Mia Lewis (11)	96
Amy Jane Clewes (10)	97
Abigail King (9)	98
Sky Kaitlin Brookes (11)	99
Teia Brown (10)	100
Aishah Ali (10)	101
Scarlett Star Timothy (9)	102
Heidi Parker (10)	103
Jaspreet Mander (11)	104

Moat Hall Primary School, Great Wyrley

Eva Nightingale (9)	105
Jarvis William Hopley (9)	106
Cameron Howell (9)	107
Tamzin Booth (10) & Abi Olivia Follows	108
Ella Louise Stanley (9)	109
Chelsea Read (11)	110
Magnus Woods (9)	111

Moorcroft Wood Primary School, Bilston

Lola Morgan (11)	112
Maisie Chloe Rae Ratcliffe (10)	113
Olivia Price (11)	114
Kyle-Reece Brookes (10)	115

Oldswinford CE Primary School, Oldswinford

Benjamin Lee Furness (9)	116
Amelia Rose Ablett (10)	117
Evie Tromans (9)	118
Olivia Dawson (9)	119
Ray Mellor (9)	120
Annabel Stark (9)	121

| Jasper Bell (10) | 122 |
| Luke Parker (9) | 123 |

Rushall Primary School, Rushall

Maisy Webb (9)	124
Riley Binks	125
Matthew Cheek (8)	126
La'myah Pink (8)	127

St Elizabeth's Catholic Primary School, Coventry

Keryane Fofana (10)	128
Kenechukwu Stephanie Osanebi (10)	129
Amber Ogblu (10)	130
Marcus Chand (9)	131
Kaisa Briella Mfasoni (10)	132
Shreya Sahota (9)	133

St Joseph's Catholic Primary School, Sutton Coldfield

Isabella Bird (7)	134
Poppy Parnham (7)	135
Lydia Eustace (8)	136
Freya James (7)	137
Anabel Katrina Eve Collins (8)	138
Yien Gao (7)	139

St Mary's Catholic Primary School, Wolverhampton

Olivia Hayes (8)	140
Carlotta Susanna Cruzada (11)	141
Aash Merin Mathew (10)	142
Zenia Dillon (10)	143
Maria Burlacu (9)	144
Petru-Rares Alin Ignatescu (9)	145
Laura Skurpel (10)	146
Holly Mary Janet Conlan (10)	147
Scarlet Grace Winters (10)	148
Lacie-Lei Thompson (9)	149
Elijah Majaducon (9)	150

Tadiwa Chikomo (9)	151
Abbie McManus (10)	152
Keira Swatman (9)	153
Lucy May Nicholas (11)	154
Cian William Walker (8)	155
Favour Erhabor (10)	156

Woodfield Junior School, Penn

Anveer Gill (9)	157
Anshpreet Kaur (9)	158
Simran Bansal (9)	159
Chloe Jayne Padley-Whiles (9)	160
Gurpej Singh (9)	161
Vinaya Rai (9)	162

THE MINI SAGAS

The Yeti's Present

It all commenced when I was in Santa's rucksack, getting prepared to be delivered to the youngster who wanted me. There were a series of emotions: I felt nervous but excited.

I was on the edge of the sleigh and it was zooming so, obviously, I fell out. I was skydiving at over 450mph. Then, I found myself on the summit of Mount Everest! I *heard it*... *saw it*... The Yeti! I screamed! Somehow, it knew my name! It exclaimed, "Finally, my present from Santa." It picked me up... then almost ate me...

Mohammed Shujad Uddin (11)

My Toy

My favourite toy is my teddy bear. He is very mysterious at night; I think he comes to life! You must think I'm very stupid but I am not. I hear strange noises at night. I thought it was me and had my ears checked at the doctors but found that they were fine! So I definitely knew it was my teddy bear. I think it talks! When I told my mum, she thought I was dumb. I suppose you think I am too but last night, I saw that my teddy was chatting to my toys!

Hasan Aamir (9)

I Looked Back

My heart was pounding. Looking back, I could see the tiger's eyes flashing ominously at me, from behind an extremely tall tree. As I stood still, there was complete silence. I looked back. I was in my room and the tiger was actually a soft teddy bear. Confused, I closed my eyes and unexpectedly felt something tugging my thick, ebony hair. Swiftly, I opened them again and it wasn't a monkey, it was a tiger! I kept my eyes open but not for much longer.

Mia DeMarco (9)

Wolf Soldier's Army Are Under Attack

"Quick, run! They're gaining on us!" said Wolf Soldier. "Down this passage!" The army went between the sofas. "Under the sofa, they will go right past us!"
Suddenly they found out they couldn't run any further. The enemy had surrounded them! "Oh no, we're trapped!" said Wolf Soldier. One of the soldiers tried to break out but it was no use.
One moment after that, Wolf Soldier had had a fantastic idea. He howled like a wolf and his voice echoed around the room. The enemy began trembling with fright and retreated. What a victory!

Abbas Hussain (9)
Al Khair Primary School, Oldbury

A Little Boy Missing

Every night, when Henry was asleep, his toys woke up to guard him. One night, the soldier toy became very distressed about Henry's empty bed. He told the other toys all about it. "Let's investigate!" said Rudy, the dinosaur.
They all nodded in agreement. Five minutes later, they all had a flashlight and they looked for clues. When they arrived at the closet there was the most adorable sight ever! Henry was asleep with his teddy, in his sleeping bag! "That's cute! I guess we found him. Let's go back to the toy box!"

Lylia Tran-Messanvi (9)
Al Khair Primary School, Oldbury

Zebra Loses His Tail

As soon as the door banged, Ziyad the zebra jumped out of the toy box. "Quick everyone, come out! We have approximately 13 minutes before the human comes back from eating his lunch!"
All the toys came out one by one. They used the dressing-up box to change into party clothes. While they played musical bumps, the toys realised that Ziyad the zebra had lost his tail. Then, they played pass the parcel and guess what happened? Terry the tiger started coughing and a tail came out of his mouth! He had eaten it! What a surprise!

Ziyad Hussain (7)
Al Khair Primary School, Oldbury

The Rise Of Street Fight

Once upon a time, there lived a boy called Jack. He lived with his mom and dad, whose names were Julie and Adam.

One day, they all went to the market and there was a store there called Street Fighter. Jack loved two fighters, their names were Ryu and Zangief. They were £500 each. Jack bought both! He brought them home and always, at night, the toys would talk to each other.

One stormy night, Zangief became jealous of Ryu. There was a big fight!

Musa Hameed (10)

Al Khair Primary School, Oldbury

The Boy And The Wish Tree

Once upon a time, there lived a boy called Alvien. He lived with his father, mother and sister. He lived next to a toy tree, that he didn't know was magical. He could have six wishes. Alvien wished for ice, robots, snow, iPads and sweets. Then something weird happened... On the sixth wish, there was a paper... It said: 'Only five wishes, no more'.
He was screaming, shouting and his face got red.

Abdelrahman Mohamed Abdelaziz (8)
Al Khair Primary School, Oldbury

The Big Bed Monster

"Time for dinner, honey!" called Mum.

"Okay coming!" replied Harry.

The Lego figures leapt into action, realising that two people were stuck. "Hurry up, get the fire brigade and get up there!" yelled the soldier. Suddenly a fire engine appeared at the foot of the ladder and the firemen began their daredevil climb. The ladder almost reached but it wasn't quite there. *Thump! Thump! Thump!* Somebody was coming up the stairs. The firemen had one more try but they couldn't quite reach. Everyone froze.

"Huh, was that how I left my toys?"

Samuel Holliday

Birchills CE Community Academy, Walsall

The Unlucky Escape!

"Argh! I don't like this!" shouted Milly, the toy doll. She and her friend, Jasmine, were on Roy's toy plane, that was controlled by a remote. Roy finally finished playing, ran to his messy bedroom and chucked the toys into his toy chest! "Ow, that hurts! I think I've broken my arm!" moaned Jasmine. It was bedtime for Roy, so he went to bed.

"Coast is clear, he's asleep!" whispered Milly, as they lifted the lid and jumped out. They were about to open the door when, *ring!* The clock turned on! Jasmine and Milly stood, frozen. "Noooo!"

Dany Joy (10)
Birchills CE Community Academy, Walsall

The Toy Warrior

"Jason!" his mom called from downstairs. Jason came running down, with toys in his hands. He wore a striped shirt; black Nike shoes and ripped jeans. His blue and turquoise cap covered his pale face and chocolate hair. "Get your bag ready, Jason!" his mom yelled. "And while you're at it, put those toys down!"

Jason dropped the toys.

"Ouch!" one of the toys screeched. Jason walked away to fetch his backpack. His mom resumed making tuna sandwiches. Jason filled his bag with stuffed toys, action dolls and Playmobil figures.

Akili Ugoeze Jahzara Howell (8)

Birchills CE Community Academy, Walsall

Unicorn Toy Valley!

The unicorn toys lived in a place called Unicorn Toy Valley. Unicorn Toy Valley was a shop in Rio, where you could buy unicorn toys.

"How can we get out of this shop?" the unicorn king asked his brave soldiers.

"I have an idea, we could run out when someone comes in!" explained the queen of unicorns.

"No, the humans can't find out we can walk and talk!" the king yelled.

The queen went out of the castle and kicked the door shut behind her. The king is still sitting on his glistening, diamond throne, thinking how to get out.

Alicja Mosek (10)
Birchills CE Community Academy, Walsall

The Great Krypton Robbery

"Here we are!" Toy Captain Jones exclaimed. They rushed along the long bridge. Soon, they came to a factory. They leapt over the barbed wall. Quickly Captain Jones and his crew, who wanted to steal the factory's kryptonite, barged through the door and split up so they wouldn't be seen.

They came to a door, where they found one another. Captain Jones whispered. They ran in and surrounded all the guards inside. Shuffling forwards, they equipped their guns and warned them, "Let us take the krypton!" They then carried the krypton home.

Haaris Ali (10)

Birchills CE Community Academy, Walsall

The Attack Of Mr Porkchop

Once, in a bedroom, Jack the Lego man and the toys were playing 'find the good soldier'. The toys couldn't find the soldier. They'd searched and searched. Just then, the evil Mr Porkchop arrived in his Transformer car. He slowly stepped out.

"Attack!" Mr Porkchop yelled, as he released his evil monkeys.

"We need to fight them!" Jack shouted. Once they'd defeated the monkeys, they destroyed the pig.

"Yay!" they shouted.

Then, the lost soldier came. "What did I miss?" So they told him about it!

Colin Mosedale (10)
Birchills CE Community Academy, Walsall

Marina And Her Ninja Friend

Once upon a time there was a princess doll, called Marina. One day, she was roaming around the woods, when she heard a rattling noise and she said, "Hello, is anybody there?"

All of a sudden, a boy came and showed his face! Marina asked for his name and he said, "My name is Edmund. What's yours?"

"Marina," she replied.

Then, a Lego dragon came to fight! Edmund took his shuriken out and slayed it!

Once they got out of the woods, they went to the palace and Edmund was turned into the most amazing knight ever.

Muskaan Ali Gufran (8)

Birchills CE Community Academy, Walsall

What Happens At Night

It was nine o'clock and it was Tim's bedtime. Just before bed, Tim had tucked all of his toys in his chest and kissed them goodnight. Tim was fast asleep when his toys revived so little did he know of what his toys were up to.

A tall soldier saluted the army, before rolling out an escape route plan. A group of senior soldiers crowded around the sheet, gawping at what they saw. A map of every nook and cranny was drawn to scale, on a diagram.

As the sun ascended, the sergeant whispered, "We'll come back tomorrow, boys, farewell!"

Sukena Naqvi (10)

Birchills CE Community Academy, Walsall

The Adventures Of Blooper

Blooper zoomed around the living room. He was a black robot and was Charlie's favourite toy. As he drove, he saw a round metal object, with a bright blue light shining out of it. Blooper touched the light, making his hand disappear. Before he could bring it back out he was sucked into the object and taken to another world! When he landed he saw a dinosaur that was eating leaves from a tree. Suddenly a group of dinosaurs running towards him caused the object to fall over and suck Blooper back into the very special place that he belonged!

Hasn Husayn (7)
Birchills CE Community Academy, Walsall

Untitled

Once upon a time, there was a princess plushie, called Princess Heart who loved hearts.
One day, she went for a walk and she met a toy dragon, who breathed out fire and had white, sharp teeth. He kidnapped Princess Heart. Suddenly a prince came to rescue Princess Heart but that wasn't the end, the door was locked and he couldn't open it. Then he found the shiny, golden key but the dragon was sleeping beside it, so the prince quickly got it and unlocked the door. It opened and they escaped. Then they lived happily ever after.

Areeba Afzal
Birchills CE Community Academy, Walsall

Bobble Arms And Sam

Bobble lived inside a toy box with his friends. One day, they tried to escape so they could play. *I need to get out,* thought Bobble. That morning, all of the toys pushed and heaved at the wooden lid of the toy box but it wouldn't lift up, so Bobble used his stretchy arms to wrap around the lock and pull it off! It wasn't long before Sam, the human, caught them. Lucky for Bobble and his friends, Sam was quite young, so he was overjoyed that his toys were alive! They soon became BFFs and were basically inseparable.

Riya Mahey
Birchills CE Community Academy, Walsall

Rosey Gets Locked

One sunny day, Lilot was going out with her friends, leaving her favourite doll and doll's house behind. Little did she know that as soon as she left the house and doll started moving.

"Is she gone yet?" whispered Rosey.

"I think so!" replied the other dolls.

"Cool, let's go and play in the dress-up room!"

"Yeah, let's go!" screamed the dolls.

As they reached the room Rosey got out her favourite costume. But she heard a sound. What was she going to do?

Mahnoor Zabair (9)

Birchills CE Community Academy, Walsall

Sophie And Her Dolly

One day, Sophie was walking in the park with her friend and she brought a doll with her. "Can I play with it please?"
"Okay." They swung it on the swing, spun it on the roundabout and pushed it down the slide.
At the end of the day... "Can I have it back now please?"
"No."
"I'm telling!"
"Okay, I will give it back to you!"
After that, they went back home and had delicious hot chocolate with marshmallows. They lived happily ever after.

Zoya Khan (8)
Birchills CE Community Academy, Walsall

The Determined Escapes

Dong! It was 9:00. Jake had gone to bed and his toy spider, Wooly, had revived... Peeping through the crack of the toy chest, Wooly found that the coast was clear. Jumping out, he called, "Sergeant, we're ready!"

Suddenly, out of the blue, a dozen spiders emerged and stood in formation! The sergeant rolled out an escape plan and showed it to his comrades. He pointed his finger from one position to the other. Finally, the crack of dawn could be seen from the window, glistening and twinkling.

Zainab Naqvi (9)

Birchills CE Community Academy, Walsall

Emily And The Mystery

Emily and her friends went to the park and took their teddies. When they were about to go on the swings, one of them saw the swing moving by itself! They did not know what was happening. It was a mystery. Who was invisible and who was on the swing?

Lilly, the eldest, went on the swing that was moving. First she stopped it, then she sat on it.

"Ouch!" screamed a mysterious voice.

"Argh!" screamed Lilly.

Emily felt something invisible... It was a ghost, a friendly ghost!

Haniyah Kousar (9)

Birchills CE Community Academy, Walsall

The Teddy And The Boy

Once, there was a lonely boy who didn't have any friends. One day, he decided to make a teddy. It took him months of building, until it was finally done! The boy was still lonely and sad, so he wished the teddy would come to life.
In the night, while the boy was asleep, there was lightning and it went through the open window! It bounced off the window and onto the teddy! When the boy woke up in the morning, the teddy could talk. The boy wasn't lonely anymore and he became very happy.

Laibah Gul (9)
Birchills CE Community Academy, Walsall

Maria And Mia

Once, there were two doll sisters, named Maria and Mia. Maria was eighteen and Mia was eight. Maria was jealous of her sister because she got everything she wanted.

Suddenly there was a storm and lightning struck! It struck so hard that Maria became evil and started to kill innocent people. She created a base and made evil gadgets to help her take over the town. Her sister had a clever plan... to have a fight.

Mia called her sister when, suddenly, the storm stopped and the evil spell wore off!

Imaan Ali Gufran (8)

Birchills CE Community Academy, Walsall

The Night The Toys Came Alive

One hectic day, in the factory, a young boy called Rayacen discovered a toy Range Rover in the corner of the factory.

The factory had closed and Rayacen was watching from behind a wall. Every single toy in the factory had come to life! It seemed like the Range Rover, that Rayacen had spotted earlier, was the head of all the toys.

The next day, more workers stayed behind and when they saw the toys come to life, they fainted in shock! They told the manager and he closed down the massive factory.

Sumaiyah Sohail (10)
Birchills CE Community Academy, Walsall

The Day The Doll Came To Life

Many years ago, a girl used to love dolls. One night, whilst she was sleeping, something moved but she didn't know what it was. She got out of bed and saw a doll move! She couldn't believe her eyes. Its eyes were bloodshot and red, her hair was tangled and her clothes were ripped. As quick as a flash, she ran back to bed and pulled the covers over herself. The next day was Christmas. She ran downstairs and couldn't wait to see what she had got. She ripped open the present and saw a doll...

Irum Wajid (9)

Birchills CE Community Academy, Walsall

Carlos, The Spanish Toy

It's Christmas Eve and Carlos is travelling all the way from Spain to London, to see if someone will buy him.

He arrives at the toyshop and just waits, staring at the other toys and thinking, *look at these toys, they are so beautiful! Everyone likes them but not me! No one is taking me home.*

After two weeks in the shop, it's Christmas Day. A little girl comes in and takes him home. When he gets home, he realises that the girl who brought him home is Spanish!

Samir Wahid (8)

Birchills CE Community Academy, Walsall

A Toy's Teller

Once there was a toy robot, that loved taking long walks down aisles of the store. The toy was named Jinko.

It was a sunny morning in his aisle when Jinko heard a loud noise from far off. *Roar!* Jinko felt brave and went to see what was making that terrible noise. It was a dinosaur, stamping its feet in the parking lot. Jinko grabbed some sticky slime from the garbage bag and stuck it under the monster's feet! It fell down with a terrible thud. Jinko saved everybody!

Georgie-Mae Poston (10)
Birchills CE Community Academy, Walsall

Untitled

A long, long time ago, there lived a boy called Tom. Tom was eight years old and had some toys that were not toys. They had special abilities... They could talk and move like normal humans. No one knew about them except the boy. Tom talked and played with them when he came back from school. He had no idea where they came from, all he knew was that they were nice and didn't harm humans. Tom cherished them so much. He promised that he'd never give them away to anyone.

Hassan Aumair
Birchills CE Community Academy, Walsall

Untitled

One day I was in Toys 'R' Us and I wanted to buy an action figure, called Buzz. I asked my mom, "Can I buy it?"
She said, "No, because you might get one on your birthday."
I was surprised, so I went home and played on my Xbox until it was my birthday.
I went to sleep one day and when I woke up and went to school I had the best day because a man who was good at gymnastics came to our school. It was my birthday and I got my Buzz figure!

Kabir Munawar (9)
Birchills CE Community Academy, Walsall

Lilly The Beautiful Doll, Emma

One beautiful afternoon, Lilly was at the toy store. She wanted to buy a doll. She was looking around and she caught a glimpse of a beautiful doll, she'd never seen a doll so stunning before! Lilly bought the doll. As soon as Lilly got home, she went to her room and played with her doll, she named it Emma. After a while, Lilly left the room and her little sister, Lucy crept in and took the doll. Lilly came and Lilly said, "Don't take the doll without asking!"

Laaibah Hussain (10)
Birchills CE Community Academy, Walsall

Adventure Of Sam The Robot

In a small neighbourhood, there was a boy called Alex. It was his birthday so his mom got him a little, cute robot. He named it Sam.

One day, when Alex went to school, Sam decided to look around Alex's room. Sam liked his new home but suddenly he heard a loud sound. It was Alex's dog! He ran as fast as he could and he found a Lego house on Alex's desk. He climbed onto the desk and pushed the Lego creation and hit the dog on the head.

Michal Kaminski (9)
Birchills CE Community Academy, Walsall

Haris' Lost Toy

Me and my friends went to the forest, to look for my toy dog pet, Freddy. "Come on lads, let's get going!" but Mikail wasn't listening to me. When we'd walked for about an hour, we came to a forest and started calling out for Freddy but suddenly we heard barking!
I called out, "Freddy, Freddy!"
As we were about to turn around, we saw a horrible giant. I told Mikail to run. We all started running home.

Haris Taj (7)
Birchills CE Community Academy, Walsall

Ruby And The Tiger

Once, in a beautiful town, lived a girl called Ruby. Ruby lived with her busy aunt, Sarah. Ruby, who lived in a new house, loved tigers. One dull morning, when Ruby was sitting on the kitchen table, she saw a cereal box torn up and ripped. Aunt Sarah ran off to work. After that, it was late and Ruby was snoozing. She suddenly woke up and saw a present! She opened it and was very surprised to see a new toy tiger!

Suba Waris (9)

Birchills CE Community Academy, Walsall

A Little Girl

One day, a little girl called Lilly was with her family. Lilly went to the forest and found a doll. She picked it up and looked around in the forest with her. Lilly went everywhere and didn't miss a single bit of the forest. Then she went back to where she found the doll but lost her family. She looked all around, but she couldn't find anymore.

Siddra Sohbat (7)
Birchills CE Community Academy, Walsall

Zeah's Mission!

One morning, Zeah woke up in her owner's bedroom. "Why am I not in the toy box?" Her owner walked inside... "Ouch!" she screamed. She'd stepped on Zeah. Then Zeah left the door open so she could find her way to the toy box. Zeah scurried through the corridor. From the corner of her eye, she could see a wooden basket but the owner's mother was coming that way! She ran to the left side. There the toy box was. "Hi!"
"Oh, hello."
"I'm the new toy here."
"Oh that's cool, are you excited?"
"Yes, my name is Izzy!"

Leher Hedge (8)
Finham Primary School, Coventry

Police Attack

One afternoon, my Lego police squad were standing in the middle of my bedroom.
"We have to escape, naughty cousin Taz is coming!" said the police boss.
"But how?" asked his assistant.
"I've got a plan!" replied the boss.
Suddenly the door was creaking so they all hid. Taz walked in and could not see any Lego police to play with. The police squad rolled out a ball, which he stepped on and fell over. As he lay on the floor he could hear the Lego police squad laughing at him, which scared him so he ran away crying.

Pravan Singh Dhesi (8)
Finham Primary School, Coventry

Fuzzy's Adventure!

One night, Fuzzy the bear got chucked from the bed. "Ow! I don't like this owner. Tomorrow I'm finding another!"
It was the morning and very early when Fuzzy quickly set off. "I really hope Ella doesn't find out!" Fuzzy could not find anywhere. He even went to a sale but nobody wanted him! Now, he was thinking, *should I go or stay?*
Ella was sleeping, she never meant to throw him on purpose. He decided to go back home to Ella's bedroom and sat there, waiting for her. Ella came in. Fuzzy was really happy!

Simran Pannu (8)
Finham Primary School, Coventry

The Great Knight Fight

Once upon a time, there was a boy whose name was Zane, or Sir Zane, as he'd just become a knight. He lived in the castle of Camelot.
In the underworld, lurked the ruler of dragons. Grim Matchstick had sworn to destroy Camelot. Now, with a new knight, it would be physically impossible but he attacked anyway. Zane wasn't ready so Grim shot a meteorite at him! Then, Grim left, leaving Camelot's knights without confidence. Zane needed training, so his instructor trained him. Zane challenged Grim to another battle and he won!

Ayaan Sarosh (8)
Finham Primary School, Coventry

When The Fox Escapes

The fox crept around. "I must be quick!" she whispered. As she tiptoed she realised that there had to be an escape! Then a human came. "Where is it?" he asked himself. Then he saw the fox. The boy put her back on the toy shelf. Then he picked something up and went away. Now it was her chance!

The fox darted back to the front door and managed to sneak out. After she ran down the street, she heard something. "Look, she's so cute, can I keep her?"

"Yes!"

They were both happy!

Lucy Fei (9)
Finham Primary School, Coventry

The Escape Of The Police

One day, Garmadon found some nindroids. He said to them, "Will you help me get out of here?"
The nindroids replied, "Yes."
Garmadon was happy. They had everything they needed. They all got parachutes and then ran and flew to the highest window. The police were waiting there so the nindroids attacked them. "Oh no!" There were two nindroids left. They pushed the window open and thought they were going to escape. The boy took them back to the old city... They hated it.

Sikander Sidhu (8)
Finham Primary School, Coventry

Bobby's Adventure!

One night, Bobby the cat was asleep. Suddenly he woke up to the noise of the Hoover! Then his owner awoke too. At that moment, Bobby's owner swung him around like he always did. "I wish I had a different owner," said Bobby. Then, he went under the bed, into Toyland.

"Hello, little creature," said a very large human. "Do you want to come home with me? I will make you some food!"

"Oh okay, giant lady thing," said Bobby.

My wish came true, after all, thought Bobby.

Kimberlie Williams (9)
Finham Primary School, Coventry

The Prince And The Princess

Once upon a time, there was a toy princess who was captured. Then a toy prince heard the news, so he decided that he had to rescue her. He put his armour on, then he jumped on his horse and shouted, "Let's go. Yeah-haw!" He was going as fast as lightning.

He got there to the castle and he shouted, "Come down, you're in safe hands!" Then, the bad toy heard him!

"Oh no!" the toy princess said.

Suddenly the toy prince woke up, killed him and then they got married.

Olivia Josephine Gregory (8)

Finham Primary School, Coventry

The Escapers

There was once an army man, called Steve. Steve wanted to find a new owner! His new owner hopefully wouldn't leave him on the floor. Steve's owner opened the window and went downstairs so the army man jumped out and ran all the way to another house. The soldier hoped that his new owner would play and look after Steve.

When his new owner woke up, he started to play with his new toy soldier. He also played with all his other toys and other board games but he accidentally knocked Steve out the window.

Jeremy Livingstone (9)
Finham Primary School, Coventry

A Horse And A Queen

There was a queen called Queen Peach. Queen Peach went into a field. She was walking a long time, then she saw a horse charging towards her, it was scary. She was running away from the horse. The horse was still charging at her. She was still running away from it. She was out of the field, she was looking at the horse. The queen went away from the field.

The next day she went back to the field. She went in the field. She was a bit scared. Then they became friends and saw each other every day.

Amelia Marie Easterlow (8)
Finham Primary School, Coventry

Adventure Of Lego Minion Named Dave

One day, a Lego minion wanted to find a new owner because his owner, Bob, kept pulling his arms and legs off. It was the morning when Dave quickly set off to find a new owner. He sat on every house's doorstep and waited but he was unwanted. He found a sale and sat there, waiting to be picked but nobody wanted him. He decided he wanted to go back home.

It was a long journey back home and it started to snow. When he got home, he went back to his Lego friends. He told them his amazing adventure.

Jack Smith (9)

Finham Primary School, Coventry

The Bear Escapes!

There was a bear called Charlie, who lived in a shop. He really loved it there, especially with his friends. His friends were his life. Suddenly, a boy came and said to his mom, "Please may I have that teddy?" The boy put Charlie in the trolley. Charlie's heart stopped and he fainted. When the boy reached home, he took Charlie in the house. When Charlie was awake he quickly went out of the boy's room and looked around... He liked the house and he decided to stay there forever.

Adonai N Peters (9)
Finham Primary School, Coventry

Tom's Escape

"Woof, woof!" shouted the dog, pushing Tom back under the bed. Tom had to think of how to get rid of the dog. He had an amazing plan...
Dogs are scared of fireworks. *Yes,* he thought, *how amazing am I! Where do I find fireworks? Oh!* He looked under the bed. "Fireworks!"
He lit them. *Whoosh! Bang!* The dog ran away. "Get out!" Tom escaped and went to find a new owner. He ran and ran to find a low doorbell, house by house.

Cameron Pal (8)

Finham Primary School, Coventry

Under The Bed!

One day, there was a bear. Then, something very bad happened. He was walking along the edge of the bed and he fell off and went under the bed! "Oh no!" he whimpered. He was really far into the bed. "Will I ever get out?" He bravely decided to climb over the socks, roll under the toy bridge, go through the fish tank and finally, after all that, he could see light. The bear ran like he had never ran before. He pulled himself onto the bed just in time for bedtime!

Archie Phillip Barriscale (9)
Finham Primary School, Coventry

The Escape!

This morning, I, Alexa Jilks, tried to escape! It all happened just like this...
My owner was playing with her friend, then I snuck out of her room and into the street. I was cold, wet and soggy. Luckily the next day, Imogen went shopping with Mum for her party stuff. She saw me, scooped me up and took me home! As soon as we got there she gave me a rinse and dry off. After that, she made me promise that I would never do anything like that ever again.

Imogen Carol Jilks (9)

Finham Primary School, Coventry

Bouncy Monkeys Escape!

One rainy day, a toy called Bouncy Monkey was cuddled up by his owner, Sofia, in the living room. Bouncy Monkey was left alone in the living room. Bouncy was sad so he went to the bedroom and started to pack. Suddenly he started going crazy because he wanted to leave and get a new owner! Sofia found Bouncy Monkey packing up. She was sad but she wanted to do what was best for him. She gave Bouncy Monkey to her friend and they were very, very happy.

Tania Goffar (8)
Finham Primary School, Coventry

The Lost Snowman

One morning a Snowgirl called Jojo had been blown away from the North Pole to Coventry. It was cold in Coventry because it was snowing. A young girl called Simran was lost and she found Jojo lost too!

They walked together and found a nice place to sleep for the night. They told stories but then Jojo said that she was from the North Pole and that she was a little upset. They went on a walk and remembered that the next day was Christmas Day!

Amrit Amy Kaur Nagra (8)

Finham Primary School, Coventry

Get Out The Room

One day, the plastic soldiers were under the bed. Suddenly the boy jumped on the bed and the soldiers' base broke. They ran out quickly and ran behind the shelf. It was night when they crept out, tried to get out but there were obstacles and there was a skateboard. They rode the board out of the room and into the kitchen. They raided the food cupboard and the milk fell on the floor. Then the people stepped on them and that was the end of them!

Josh M (8)
Finham Primary School, Coventry

Lego Ninjago Escape Disaster!

One day there was a Lego figure, called Lloyd. He was a ninja. He wanted to escape the toy store, so he stormed it at night.

In the middle of the next night, Lloyd woke up and rode the Lego dragon! He flew to the security room and opened the doors. He got out but saw the owner of the toy store. Lloyd flew away on the dragon but the owner was too fast, so he and the dragon hid. Then the doors opened. They waited, then flew out!

Danyal Uddin (8)
Finham Primary School, Coventry

Freedom

Once, there was a water camera who wanted to escape from the bedroom. The water camera was trying to escape by jumping, then he tried to climb out of the room. He climbed onto the bed, then up the wall. Then, when he got to the window, the water camera just jumped. It bounced back into the room, so it decided to get out by using the front door. It ran down the stairs, and went through the front door and had a really good day!

Dylan Williams (9)
Finham Primary School, Coventry

Untitled

One lovely day, there were lots of Lego people and they really wanted to escape the bedroom. They couldn't escape because they were locked in a box! When they tried to escape, they always got caught and got put back in the box. When they got back in the box, they were very angry and they wanted to get out of the smelly, old box. When they got out again, they ran out of the door and they were free forever, hooray!

Flynn Mold (8)
Finham Primary School, Coventry

Viva La Revolution!

"Viva la revolution!" cried the dog teddy. "Load the cannon!"

"We hate humans bossing us around, we will fight back!" shouted the soldier. The toys loaded the toy gun.

"We will have to wait until bedtime to attack," cried Bailey, the rabbit. Suddenly, footsteps started to ring in their eardrums.

"Men, in formation! Fight for your rights!" commanded the general.

The dog teddy bellowed, "On my command. Three, two, one!" The door burst open. *Pop!* The gun went off.

"Ahh, my leg!" roared the boy. "Wait, what's this?" It fell silent.

"Are you okay dear?" called his mum.

James Wade (11)
King Henry VIII Preparatory School, Coventry

The Search For A New Abode

"Seatbelts on, crossed fingers for hope!" Jack called out to his crew. The spaceship was about to land and the rocket was zooming like a meteor. "Rocket one, one, triple four, is about to land, Captain!" Rachel called out. "In three, two, one..." There was a thud, with smoke hitting the planet's ground. Lined behind each other they hopped onto the planet's surface as hooded figures towered menacingly over them. They communicated telepathically with the hooded figures. "Could this be our new home?" Jack asked.
"Maybe," the unknown creatures said. This could've been the answer to it!

Akanksha Linesh (10)
King Henry VIII Preparatory School, Coventry

The Dinosaur Quest

One magical night, when a boy snuggled in bed, his toy dinosaurs came to life! Cuddly, a young dinosaur, realised his friend, Alamo, the alamosaurus, was missing. "Alamo, where are you?" yelled Cuddly.

After some frantic searching, Cuddly caught sight of Alamo's tail under the boy's duvet. So he gathered all the dinosaurs to create a plan, to retrieve Alamo! The dinosaurs decided to distract the boy, whilst Cuddly was tasked with retrieving Alamo.

"Hooray!" came a voice. "Alamo is back again!" Cuddly had successfully united Alamo back with the group and they enjoyed all night playing together.

Haresh Raguram (9)

King Henry VIII Preparatory School, Coventry

Lost

Every day, Lila, the toy elephant, gazed longingly out of the window. "I wish I could go outside," she sighed to herself.

One morning, as Optricia left for work, Lila snuck out, following her owner. Optricia didn't notice Lila right behind her, even as she returned home that evening.

For weeks, Lila had this same adventure.

WOW!

The outside world was brilliant. Before long, Lila got bored. When the outside world was not so brilliant, Lila decided to go home early. Soon, she was lost! Lila begged for help but nobody would listen!

After all, everyone knows toys can't talk!

Amba Bodali-Bosson (8)
King Henry VIII Preparatory School, Coventry

Jim And Jeff

A pair of toy twins, Jim and Jeff, woke up on a bright summer's day. "How are you today, Jim?" said Jeff.

"Fine," said Jim. They went off to steal from Tom's secret stash of sweets. Their casual stroll was soon interrupted by a rumble, not any rumble though. Suddenly, the door creaked open.

"Knew it!" said Jeff. "Tom's come back for some more sweets!"

"Come on, lie down!" They suddenly flopped to the ground and acted dead. As soon as Tom was gone, they dashed off and robbed Tom's precious secret stash of sweets, chocolate and crisps!

Oliver Wang (10)

King Henry VIII Preparatory School, Coventry

Checkmate!

"Sire, we have broken through their defence!" shouted the gold rook. The gold king looked at the position and saw his chance to defeat the silver king, with one last clever combination.

"Bishop move in line with our queen!" ordered the gold king, as his troops got into position to attack. The bishop moved diagonally to his queen, as she took a breath and realised that victory was down to her.

The queen then moved quickly to capture the pawn that was protecting the silver king, before planting the fatal kiss of death on the silver king. "Checkmate!" said Magnus.

Arjun Vadgama (8)

King Henry VIII Preparatory School, Coventry

Toilet Trouble

Ted's bristled, brown fur shook, as he looked forward at the colossal door, that lay rooted to the soft, luxurious carpet. As soon as he had squeezed through the minuscule crack in the door, Ted stood open-mouthed in awe, as he stared around. When sense finally slapped him awake, the door had slithered shut. Ted, the teddy bear, was trapped! Ted yelled in fright, as a wet-nosed bulldog shuffled towards him. Terrified he leapt above the toilet, grabbing the soft toilet roll, which started to slowly unwind! *Splash!* Water leapt gracefully out of the toilet, as he fell in.

Silvia luga (10)
King Henry VIII Preparatory School, Coventry

Board Game Or Adventure

A plastic cube thundered across the board with six, black, hollow holes of emptiness placed on top. A gargantuan hand plucked me off the land. I struggled to get free! It dropped me back down to the ground. *Boom, boom, boom!* A snake-like monster charged into the chamber, no one could defeat it! No one except me. I focused my spirit into my trembling hand and shot a fireball at the thing. It hit it square in the torso and it toppled over. Dead. "I win, I win!" I, Mike the Marvellous, was victorious once again.

Himmat Singh Chana (10)

King Henry VIII Preparatory School, Coventry

The Great Sacrifice

"Get me out of here!" cried Barbie, struggling to get out of a web in a haunted attic. Suddenly, spiders started appearing. They were almost on her! Luckily, the hero of all time, Octo Man grabbed her and put her in Speedy's boot. Quickly, they rode into a hole. They thought they were safe but huge rats appeared.

"Argh!" They all screamed and scarpered. Speedy grabbed everyone and put them in his boot! Octo Man jumped out and with all his strength, lifted the attic door and let the toys out! From then on, Octo Man was a legend.

Sukhmani Kaur (10)
King Henry VIII Preparatory School, Coventry

The Teddy Bear's Christmas Wish

There was once a teddy bear that nobody cared about. His owner would kick him, the dog would bite him and the owner's friend would drown him when playing with him.

One day, the teddy bear finally had enough, "I will ask Santa to make people like me for Christmas!" he said. So that's what he did.

On Christmas Day, nothing happened - everything was the same as usual. But the next day, the owner gave him to charity which led him to a poor girl, who'd been wishing for a teddy bear all year! He then lived happily ever after.

William He (9)

King Henry VIII Preparatory School, Coventry

T-Rex And His Friends

One morning, in a land far away, a T-rex and his friends went out to play because it was sunny!
"Can we play hide-and-seek?" said Harry to one of the other dinosaurs.
"Toilet tag!" said Ellie, another dinosaur, happily.
Lastly, T-rex said, "The floor is lava!"
"The floor is lava!" said the other dinosaurs.
"I made it on my own!" said T-rex. T-rex just turned around and saw the wicked, old dinosaur. They ran and she chased them. They ran until the dinosaur was completely tired.

Xanthe Wong (7)
King Henry VIII Preparatory School, Coventry

Haunted!

Without a care in the world, Jinny hummed to herself as she neared Gumbletrip Manor. Outside was a smartly dressed man. He beckoned her in. Now out of the sunshine, Jinny shivered and her floral dress brushed against cobwebs. She was drawn towards an old oak table in the middle of the room. There sat a doll, with strange, button eyes. In a slightly menacing tone, it asked, "Do you want to play?"

Jinny wanted to run but it was too late. The doll's hypnotic gaze had drawn her into its power. Now, two dolls sat at the oak table.

Eloise Mills (11)

King Henry VIII Preparatory School, Coventry

Adventures In Candy Land

We saw a sign saying: 'Candy Land' with sugar water drops dripping. I opened the huge gate and out came the smell of bubblegum, chocolate, fizzy sherbet and marshmallows, so lovely. The floor was sticky with sweet strawberry syrup. We walked towards colourful grass and I tried a blue blade. It was the most amazing, strawberry, crackling sweet that I have ever tasted. Love heart bubbles started popping out of my ears.

Suddenly I heard, "It's time to get up!" It was a dream. It was really fun being Glowy, my teddy bear.

Aman Marwaha (7)
King Henry VIII Preparatory School, Coventry

The Man With The Bloody Finger

There was a girl called Lucy who was on her phone, texting. Suddenly she got a message saying: 'Hello, I am the man with the bloody finger and I am at your street'.

The same time next day, she was on her computer and it said: 'I am at your house'.

Next morning, Lucy got a message saying: 'Hello I am the man with the bloody finger and I am at your bedroom door!'

Lucy opened the door and saw a doll. "Hello, I am the man with the bloody finger, may I have a plaster for my finger please."

Raveena Dave

King Henry VIII Preparatory School, Coventry

Quacky, My Duck

I've got a little toy duck called Quacky. He's very cheeky and he can talk and walk like any human. I love my little Quacky! I'm going to tell you a story about him.

One day, Quacky decided to set up a detective agency with my other toy, Piglet! "Noodle Detective Agency!" said Quacky, when the phone rang.

"Hey, that's not the name we agreed on!" argued Piglet.

Just then a voice spoke on the phone... It was Mummy! Donald explained that they were in the middle of a detective agency!

Aanya Kachhala (10)
King Henry VIII Preparatory School, Coventry

The Teddy Which Comes Alive

One day, there was a boy called Dexter. He was sleeping, then out the corner of his eye, he saw the giant teddy, dancing, prancing and leaping around! Dexter decided to follow the teddy. He went to the kitchen, where there were more teddies! Each room he went to had even more teddies, dancing. By the time they were in the garden there were 1,000 teddies. Suddenly they leapt into a bush and were transported to a different world. Dexter wanted to follow them but he knew he was going to miss his mum and dad, so he didn't go.

Sian Madahar (8)

King Henry VIII Preparatory School, Coventry

The Dilemmas Of A Teddy Bear!

She hurts me every day. I wish she knew how much it hurts. She chews my ear. Is she a giraffe? She says I smell but she smells more! Yet it's my head spinning in the washing machine! That woman thinks I'm her pillow, not her friend! Travelling... Don't get me started on that! I get kicked off the chair and onto the floor and she only looks for me when she needs a friend. Strange, despite all this, she tells everybody that I'm her best friend. She takes me everywhere, only bothering to speak on the way home!

Kiran Heer (9)
King Henry VIII Preparatory School, Coventry

The Twisted Pink Horse

There once was a gaudy, pink horse whose name was Cobalt. The horse's dream was to play Twister. Cobalt was a flexible toy; there are pros and cons to being a flexible toy but in Twister, it's neither! Cobalt has a habit of tripping over his tail a lot. You see, he has a very long tail.

On his birthday, he received a Twister mat. Of course, he played and he was literally tied up. The horse was now a knot! Once he'd clumsily untangled himself, his long tail was gone and now has a horn on his head!

Mara Iuga (11)

King Henry VIII Preparatory School, Coventry

The Story Of Cat Heroes

There was a cat. The cat saw some food but it was banned! The cat ate all of it and became Purry Puncher! He fought against crime. Purry Puncher went to the pet store and he bought a cat. The two cats walked outside, happily. The little cat saw some food but it was banned. The little cat ate it all up and became Pluffy Tails! A heroic duo formed. They were cat heroes! They were great. One day, a robber was in a bank but the cat heroes were there! They beat him up! "Miaow!" they happily cheered.

Atharva Karn (9)
King Henry VIII Preparatory School, Coventry

Friendship Wins The Day!

One day, in a toyshop, a unicorn came alive. A lot of dolls came to life as well. The dolls came together as a big army, with the unicorn in charge. There was an evil toy dog and the unicorn and her army were trying to defeat it. They had a Barbie doll, with sharp high heels to stab it with. They went to find him at midnight, when he would be asleep. But the dog was awake and waiting for them. "I don't want to fight!" he said. He had realised he'd rather have friends than enemies.

Lucy Wade (9)

King Henry VIII Preparatory School, Coventry

A Strange Soft Toy

One day, a kind lady gave me a cute, soft toy cat. It was skinny, with bright, golden, crispy eyes. She told me to feed the cat that I called Harmony, which I thought was a joke but she looked deadly serious! So I left food for the toy cat and to my surprise, it looked hungry and crawled steadily, towards the food. To my amazement, it ate in front of my eyes. I stood as still as a statue and froze in astonishment. I hugged Harmony, remembering what my mum said - that I already had way too many toys.

Anastasia O'Neill (9)

King Henry VIII Preparatory School, Coventry

The Reindeer Who Lost His Nose

The clock struck twelve but there was nothing to be heard. Everyone was asleep, except for one girl. Suddenly there was a thud, the girl could hear a rumbling on the roof tiles. She looked out of her bedroom window to see a red nose, glowing in the snow below. Silently, she ran downstairs and out into the cold. She picked up the wet, warm nose, looked up and saw a reindeer on the roof. Without thinking, she threw the nose high into the air. The reindeer flew and caught it, then winked and was gone!

Gabriella Olivia Duggan (9)
King Henry VIII Preparatory School, Coventry

My Awesome Sid

Sid got bored. He planned to get out of the toyshop. On the night of 8th September, he squeezed past his sleeping brothers and sisters. He pushed lots of board game boxes onto the floor. The automatic doors opened and Sid ran out of the shop. He climbed his very first tree. He was a little afraid of heights, but soon he got used to it. He started to enjoy it. Did I ever tell you who Sid is? His tail is all fuzzy and he is dark brown. He is my favourite cuddly squirrel!

Hannah Alijan Kazmi (9)
King Henry VIII Preparatory School, Coventry

The Snowman Who Lost His Body

One morning, I woke up to see snow outside. My cousins came round and we all made a snowman! It took hours to make. We decided to make the body first, by rolling the snow into a great big ball. Then we made the snowman's head, by rolling a smaller ball. We then proceeded to place the head on top of the body. We added sprouts for the eyes and a carrot for the nose. Then, later in the day, the sun came out and it started to rain. The snowman started to melt!

Alexa Duggan (8)

King Henry VIII Preparatory School, Coventry

The Red Ruby

One dark night, Samantha snuggled up in her bed, waiting for her mum to tuck her in. As soon as Samantha fell asleep, her big toddler-sized unicorn woke. Because of the dark night, her eyes were like blue diamonds, glittering in the night's sky. The unicorn's name was Ruby. Ruby suddenly clambered out of the window, fluttering like a diamond in the air. Ruby gently landed on the cold and icy, frozen pavement. Suddenly, she spotted a shining red light on the pavement. Ruby clutched the red light and fluttered back home. Would she ever be found?

Amirah Thompson (10)
Lote Tree Primary School, Foleshill

The Awakening Of The Toys

One sparkling, shimmering day, all the toys in the kingdom came to life. They had fallen asleep for a hundred years! A spell had been cast on them by a wicked wizard. Princess Plum asked her fabulous father, "Dad, are you okay?"

The king replied, "I'm fine, honey." The king and Princess Plum glanced out of the window and looked at the kingdom. They realised that the ferocious fire-breathing dragon was awake! The king suddenly told everyone and tried to calm them. He and his loyal people thought of an impeccable idea!

Maryam Haroon (10)

Lote Tree Primary School, Foleshill

Vacoona The Vicious Vampire Toy

On a furious night, a little vampire named Vacoona was stomping in her cave. Vacoona was a toy, a very mischievous toy. When her mother wasn't around, she liked to gobble up innocent, plastic bats. "I want to eat Hulk," said Vacoona, so she went to the next aisle to find him. First, she checked if her mother was around. Then, Hulk woke up.

"Vacoona, what are you doing?"

Crunch! Crunch! Who next? Oh, Spider-Man! Crunch!

"Bye Spider-Man!" The janitor came and stomped on Vacoona!

Fahmida Begum (10)

Lote Tree Primary School, Foleshill

A Secret In The Night

Teddy bears seem so harmless but when the sun goes down, it's another story! When children are asleep, they awaken. They climb out of your house and go to a certain part of the forest called, 'The Death'. They fight to their deaths and the losers get thrown into the darkness of the night. Once, one teddy bear won at least five rounds. They were having a competition to see who could become king. Once you're king, you can do anything! They return back home and kill the humans. If you have a teddy bear, throw it out!

Isa Khaleel (10)
Lote Tree Primary School, Foleshill

The Emerald Necklace

One shiny morning, Emily woke up with a magnificent smile on her face. She jumped out of bed. Emily felt the excitement in her, it was her birthday! Emily ran downstairs and saw her mum and dad. She saw huge presents wrapped up. She leapt to them, shaking the boxes to feel what was inside. She opened one, it was an emerald-green necklace. She put it on as she opened another present. She saw her teddy walking up to her with scissors as sharp as swords! Emily moved back, there was nowhere to go...

Safiya Snaaullah (10)

Lote Tree Primary School, Foleshill

Arcade Comes To Life

As soon as it struck 11:30, Simon was getting all his supplies ready in his military bag so he could meet his friends at the arcade, play games and have fun.

Once it was 12, Simon and his friends were just about to walk outside. Suddenly, the door shut on them and the machine turned on, trying to grab Simon with its wires! On the other side, his friend was trying to bust the door open while his other friend was taking cover from basketballs...

Ismaeel Yousuf (10)

Lote Tree Primary School, Foleshill

A Jungle Journey!

"Boss, where are you?" the toy truck called as he climbed over heaps of sand.
"I don't know, it's a big jungle you know!"
"Okay, calm down," the truck replied.
The truck passed many trees, which towered over him like a tribe of toy monkeys! "There you are, you silly billy!" shouted the boss.
As they argued, screeching and whispering came from the other side of the jungle. "What's that?" asked the truck.
"Dunno, let's have a look!" replied the boss, excitedly.
They arrived at a dark, mysterious cave. "Let's check it out!" the boss said.
"O-okay," replied the truck.

Tonisha Malhi (11)
Moat Farm Junior School, Oldbury

How Unicorns Came To Life!

Once upon a time, there was a magical toy lying on the pavement. It wasn't just any toy... it was special, very special. It was rainbow, fluffy and very glittery. A girl, called Vina, saw it on the streets. She screamed, "OMG, Mum! Look, there's a toy over there. It's a unicorn!" gasped Vina.

"Vina, okay, okay! Calm down, it's not yours!" said Mom.

"But please, pretty please."

"Fine, just calm down."

The next day, Vina took it to school to show her best friend, Rayiah. Rayiah loved it! They both turned around... There was a real unicorn!

Vina Hassan (10)
Moat Farm Junior School, Oldbury

A Monster Under The Bed!

"Argh! Where am I?" Nathaniel the toy action figure was under the bed. Nathaniel looked around and saw something big, very big... Much bigger than him! Nathaniel was shocked and confused, first he thought, *if I stay here the monster won't wake up*, however, Nathaniel was scared. So, as quietly as he could, he escaped from the bed. "Yes, I escaped! It smelt under there!" Nathaniel tiptoed as silently as he could to the toy box and tried to get up. Little did he know, that Remarn was watching him.
Shocked, Remarn screamed, "Mom, Dad, come here!"

Remarn Taylor (10)
Moat Farm Junior School, Oldbury

The Lost Friend

Once upon a time, there was a boy called Harry and two more boys called Jayden and Amrit. All they did was play hide-and-seek. Aeshveer said, "I'm going to hide and you two are it!"
They both said, "Okay."
They counted from ten to one. Aeshveer found a forest and went in deep to hide. Immediately, they found his footprints, that lead to the forest. "Oh no!" they said. "This is a problem."
They went to the depths of the forest. They found Aeshveer and a bear! They ran out of the forest and to a random home...

Aeshveer Maan
Moat Farm Junior School, Oldbury

Jo In The Box

Once upon a time, in a lost world, lived toys. But not just any toys... Toys that could come to life! Barbie was forever friends with Jack. Jo, who was Jack's sister, liked to scare people.
Late one night, she went to Jack and suddenly... "Boo!"
"What did you do that for?"
"To teach Jo a lesson!"
Barbie and Jack decided to scare her. They crept quietly over while she was sleeping and... "Boo!" They scared Jo. Her face was white. "What was that for?"
She promised she would stop.

Willow Harmony Moore (9)
Moat Farm Junior School, Oldbury

Rags To Riches

Tucked away in the corner of the toy box, lived a solemn ragdoll, called Ruby. Mia, her owner, had neglected her for years. Deciding to make some money, Mia's mom went into Mia's toy box, found various toys, including her ragdoll.

The day of the sale arrived and lots of families attended. Falling in love, a little girl called Phoebe picked up Ruby and purchased her. When they got home, Ruby got washed, dried and her dress sewn, to make her look as good as new. Ruby and Phoebe played together every day. Ruby really went from rags to riches!

Faith Abigail Green (9)

Moat Farm Junior School, Oldbury

That Friday Night...

It all happened on Friday. I sat on Sumayyah's bed, when suddenly, a flash of light appeared. Once I opened my eyes, I looked up to see apps. What really scared me was the fact that I was in the computer! I remembered I had watched a movie about this and I had to travel through the wires! I tucked up and crawled through. I twirled through the wires and ended up on the desk! "What?" exclaimed Sumayyah, my owner. "How did you get here?" If only she saw the journey I had on Friday night.

Sumayyah Aliyah Mahmood (11)
Moat Farm Junior School, Oldbury

A Day At The Beach

The day when me and my owner, Lucy, witnessed a whale, was one I will never forget. Let me tell you how it all happened.
As the sun rose with a cool breeze, a gentle swish of golden sand blew quickly through the air. Proudly, the lonely palm trees stood, hovering over the never-ending blue. Unexpectedly, I saw the whale. We went closer to get a better view. There it was! It had a box-like head, huge, cone-shaped teeth, small flippers and a little hump on its back. I absolutely could not believe my eyes...

Rayiah Hussain (10)
Moat Farm Junior School, Oldbury

Aundrea Dream

Waiting for the shop to close, the lights to go out and the alarm to go beep, Aundrea peeked out from the corner of the box. She wished that some day soon, she would be chosen to go to a special home, along with the caravan accessory. Unfortunately, the next day, the Lego caravan had run out of stock. She felt overwhelmed with sadness at not being picked! Maybe tomorrow her dream will come true!

The next day, she was picked and lived in a happy home with all of her Lego friends.

Mia Lewis (11)
Moat Farm Junior School, Oldbury

Maisy The Magic Ragdoll

Maisy was a ragdoll but not an ordinary ragdoll...
She was magic. Every time her owner left, Maisy's
nose would start twitching. Her fingers would
move slowly and she started to blink! One day,
Maisy got up and explored the house, curiously,
with joy. She feared running into someone. What if
someone saw her? What would she do? Would she
fall limp to the floor or would she run and hide?
It actually happened one day and Maisy was
shocked, so she ran and hid but her owner found
her.

Amy Jane Clewes (10)
Moat Farm Junior School, Oldbury

My Unicorn Adventure

I was sleeping but woke up to see my unicorn, Ted, sitting and looking at me. She said, "We are going on an adventure."
Before I knew it, I was on her back, flying through the sky. We flew under stars and over clouds until we got to a magical land, where she came from. She showed me around and we had fun running over rainbows and rolling down hills. We sat on soft grass to rest for a bit, before it was time to go. We flew back home and I fell asleep, Mom soon woke me up.

Abigail King (9)
Moat Farm Junior School, Oldbury

The Cookie Craver

Gizmo was an adorable stuffed bunny. He had lost an eye and half an ear but wasn't evil like the children suspected. Years of love had worn him out. His only fault was that he craved cookies... far too much.

Gizmo had a dark secret; once a year, he came to life. Having not eaten for a year, he was dragged by his craving into the kitchen. Soon enough, Gizmo goes insane, smashing until it looked like a bomb had hit. After being demolished, the kitchen surrendered... A cookie!

Sky Kaitlin Brookes (11)
Moat Farm Junior School, Oldbury

The Magic Nutcracker Doll

Once upon a time, there was a girl called Ella. Ella had a wish and that wish was to have a Christmas. She had never had a Christmas before. On Christmas Eve, she was walking on the road and she found a Nutcracker doll but it was magic! So she told the doll her wish, then went back home to bed.

Overnight the doll decorated the room and gave Ella presents, so Ella wouldn't be devastated this year!

She woke up in shock, opened all of her presents and played in the snow!

Teia Brown (10)
Moat Farm Junior School, Oldbury

Lost In The Snow!

Once upon a time there lived a girl called Rosie, who woke up and saw snow. Her mum told her to leave Teddy, so she put him on a window sill. Without notice her mum banged the window. Poor Teddy flew over the washing line, and landed on the snow! Teddy got up and slipped on a piece of wood, then down a hill.

He started playing with snow. He tried to go home but he was lost! Suddenly a sleigh came and took him home through the chimney. It was Santa! Teddy went to bed.

Aishah Ali (10)
Moat Farm Junior School, Oldbury

The Big Dreamer

Hello, I'm Marcus. I'm here to tell you my story. It all started when I fell asleep in my toy store. Then somebody bought me. I was so ecstatic! A few minutes later I was unboxed. Their house was colossal! They even had a room for me. Who would think I was going to be unboxed! Why did they pick me?
Suddenly I fell asleep. I did feel a bit drowsy after being played with. Unfortunately, when I woke up I was back in the store.I guess I'm just a big dreamer!

Scarlett Star Timothy (9)
Moat Farm Junior School, Oldbury

The Mysterious Dragon Toy

Once, there lived a boy who lived in a village with his mom and dad. One day, they went to a toyshop to buy Danny a toy. In the shop he saw a toy dragon, so they bought it.

When they got home, Danny played with his dragon and then it disappeared. So he tried to search for it but it wasn't there!

A week later, the dragon was found and it turned into a real dragon! Then, Danny had to try to turn it back to a normal dragon and he did.

Heidi Parker (10)

Moat Farm Junior School, Oldbury

Lost In A Concert

I jumped up and down with excitement. It was my
first time in London and going to a concert. I heard
the loud chime of Big Ben. Our journey had just
begun. *Music*, I thought, as we entered. Katie, my
friend, ran quickly and I lost my grip and fell!
All I could see was feet. Somebody picked me up. It
was Katie, she had found me. After the concert
was finished, Katie and I travelled back home to
have a nice, hot cup of tea.

Jaspreet Mander (11)
Moat Farm Junior School, Oldbury

The Living Doll!

"Emma, wake up!" Mum called.

"Okay, Mum!" Emma said, yawning. She climbed out of bed and looked in the mirror. "Argh!" Emma screamed.

"What's wrong?" her mum yelled up the stairs.

"I'm a doll!" Emma lifted her arms and legs. "Ouch! I'm super stiff!" she exclaimed. She was in a cute little dress and her hair was in two pigtails with a red bow either side. "Whoa, I look different!" she said, spinning.

She started playing with army figures and dolls when suddenly, she turned back to her normal self. "Argh!" she said, solemnly. "That was fun!"

Eva Nightingale (9)

Moat Hall Primary School, Great Wyrley

The Fish Attack

"Danny!" shouted Harry.

"Yeah!" Danny cried back.

"Is the boat ready?"

Danny nodded his head and Harry climbed on. The little people pretended that the carpet was the sea. But Harry, however, thought he needed something more daring and dangerous. "Hey Danny, I think we should do something more dangerous!" called Harry.

"Okay if you insist," said Danny, who was happily going with the flow.

They climbed up onto the cupboard without making a sound. Eventually, they got a plastic dingy. Danny jumped in and from nowhere, a Lego shark came!

Jarvis William Hopley (9)
Moat Hall Primary School, Great Wyrley

Jeff And The Lego Figure

"This is really hard work," Jeff sighed, "I wish I was a faster builder." Jeff was in a child's bright and colourful bedroom. Whilst building his house, Jeff heard a creak. He realised it was a human! "Oh no, a human is coming. He's going to destroy my house! I've got to hide!" Jeff cried. He shot off to hide from the massive human.

"What's this? I'd better destroy it and put it back!" the human said.

He walked out, forgetting to shut the door. After another hour, he'd finished his build, he decided to make a cosy, soft bed.

Cameron Howell (9)
Moat Hall Primary School, Great Wyrley

Sleep With One Eye Open...

"Must be quiet. Can't be seen," the ragdoll whispered, crawling out from under the bed, when all of a sudden, darkness enveloped the room, blinding the ancient toy's vision! "How dare she throw me under the bed then blind me!" she spat, searching for a weapon to get revenge. On the floor, she spotted a pair of rusty old scissors. With all of her anger, the ragdoll picked up the scissors and darted up the bed. She approached the girl's face, shadows dancing around her. The doll stopped, the light flicked on and the girl stared at her...

Tamzin Booth (10) & Abi Olivia Follows

Moat Hall Primary School, Great Wyrley

Billy And The Fishy Mystery!

I am starving! thought Billy, the seal. He was sitting on my bedside table, staring into space. "I must get food!" he said.

I was fast asleep, dreaming of unicorns, so I didn't hear him creeping down the stairs. He pushed open the living room door, to find it empty. He waddled over to the fridge and, *bang!* "Oh no!" Billy shouted.

I jumped out of bed and dashed down the stairs. I ran into the kitchen, to find Billy lying on his back, next to a smashed can of fish! I screamed, "Mum! Look what Billy has done now!"

Ella Louise Stanley (9)
Moat Hall Primary School, Great Wyrley

Happiness At Last!

One quiet night, in Chelsea's cosy bedroom, Michael Blue Mouse, the teddy, suddenly came alive. His eyes were golden sunshines, his ears were pink, yellow and as soft as velvet. His precious, blue fur shone in the moonlight. Loudly, Chelsea was snoring, so didn't notice a thing. All day, Chelsea had wanted to talk to someone and Michael was about to make that happen! Strangely, Michael got sucked through an iPad and programmed a soul. Soon, he teleported with the soul, back through the iPad. Then he woke up Chelsea and started a jolly, happy conversation!

Chelsea Read (11)
Moat Hall Primary School, Great Wyrley

Red's Adventure... Sorta

I am Red. I escaped my owner, Dan, who threw me into a wall. I launched myself out of an open window and landed in a roasting pool, inside a cave but it was actually a spaniel's mouth! I jittered about until it coughed me up. I rolled through a small gap in the wooden fence and onto the cold pavement. I dodged in-between feet until a coin squashed me. Me and the coin got taken into a small house. Well back to the drawing board, literally.

Magnus Woods (9)

Moat Hall Primary School, Great Wyrley

How A Unicorn Grew Its Horn

"She looks so weird," whispered Sparkle the unicorn.

"I know, right?" muttered Crystal, but little did they know, Lexi the unicorn (who they had been talking about) was listening! They were talking about her because Lexi didn't have a horn.

When she was walking home, she saw an abandoned toy car. Eventually, she got home and darted past her parents and went to the bathroom. She started washing the car and it looked as good as new! Lexi felt weird... She had grown a horn! It must have been because she was helping others with cars!

Lola Morgan (11)
Moorcroft Wood Primary School, Bilston

Just Wish

On one Christmas Eve, a young girl asked her mother and father if she could get a teddy bear for Christmas. She wrote a note to Santa saying: 'Santa, I don't want a lot for Christmas. All I want is a teddy bear, with curly hair. That will mean a lot to me, from Chelsea'.

Chelsea posted her letter and went to sleep. Then, she heard the door open. Snow crunched and then the door slammed, she thought it was nothing. When she woke up, by the tree was a teddy bear with curly hair like she'd always wanted.

Maisie Chloe Rae Ratcliffe (10)

Moorcroft Wood Primary School, Bilston

Fairy Party

Once upon a time, one sunny morning, I woke up with a tingly feeling in my toy fairy toes. I remembered right away why it was such a special day. In a few minutes, with the help of a little magic, I had combed my hair, brushed my teeth and washed my toy wings. My name is Breeze; I am a messenger fairy toy! Nobody notices messenger fairies very much.

Olivia Price (11)
Moorcroft Wood Primary School, Bilston

The Story Of The Christmas Elf On The Shelf

This is a story of a Christmas elf. One day in December, an elf came to life but only at night, when everyone was asleep in bed.

The next day was Christmas Eve. The elf knew Santa would be there that night! The elf went and sat on the shelf. He got bored and jumped off the shelf, to go and explore...

Kyle-Reece Brookes (10)

Moorcroft Wood Primary School, Bilston

Wild Warfare

When Samuel leaves his home he doesn't know that his toys come to life or that his cat, Purrkins, is a secret weapon for the Animal Nation Army.
"Coast is clear! Wild warfare! You knuckleheads, get into defensive formations!" yelled Sergeant Fuzzy, of the Animal Nation Army.
General Furious, leader of the Strictlock Army shouted, "Attack!"
Foam bullets started flying everywhere. Animal Nation was struggling under heavy fire. Then Purrkins pounced in and, *bam!* as she swooshed her tail and knocked Strictlock clean off the battle floor. Animal Nation victory!
"Code red! Samuel!" screamed Fuzzy. Everyone resumed toy position.

Benjamin Lee Furness (9)
Oldswinford CE Primary School, Oldswinford

A Scare For Frasier Bear

As Frasier Bear struggled onto the plush, mountainous bed, he heard the thumping of feet on the rickety, ancient staircase. "Oh no!" he whispered. "Grace is coming!" He shuffled over to the toy pile but they couldn't make enough room for him! There was only one thing he could do... Frasier Bear tried to heave the soft blanket over his cotton head but he was too late!
As the door to the bedroom creaked open, Frasier fell to the floor with a gentle bump, feeling extremely anxious. "Frasier?" Grace exclaimed, as she nervously moved nearer to the motionless, silent bear.

Amelia Rose Ablett (10)

Oldswinford CE Primary School, Oldswinford

The Secret Life Of Toys

"Alright toys, let's get this party started!" cried the captain of the toys.
Toys swarmed in and began having fun. They pulled open the fridge and began messing around. Dolls bounced on jelly, like it was a trampoline. Teddies made paw marks in the butter and then dipped it in sugar and ate it gleefully! Plastic army men pulled off the corks of champagne bottles and made themselves fly through the air. Lego people swam very happily in the sink until... "Ouch!" cried Theo, as he stepped on a doll. He stared at the toys. The game was up!

Evie Tromans (9)
Oldswinford CE Primary School, Oldswinford

The Night Sylvanian Families Came To Life!

One night, when Olivia was sleeping, her Sylvanian families came to life. They crept downstairs, into the kitchen and stole chocolate and cake for their journey to Legoland.
They travelled high and low and met Hugo, Olivia's cat and travelled on his ginger back. Then, they went to Legoland and got off Hugo's back. They walked in and it was amazing! The sun started to rise and Olivia awoke. They ran back to Beechwood Hall just in time, before Olivia woke up! They thought to themselves, *that was the most amazing night ever!*

Olivia Dawson (9)
Oldswinford CE Primary School, Oldswinford

Lego Larry's Night-Time Adventure

One midnight, Lego Larry jumped onto Ryan's bed. It looked like a mountain! The covers were like frosty, cold snow. He could also see Ryan sleeping. Larry slid down the mountain-like covers, falling, falling until he hit the ground, with a thump. He was losing ground when suddenly he peered round the corner. He thought to himself, *let's go on an adventure!*

Larry sprinted under the door and looked down the stairs. He was on the edge of the stairs when he tripped and fell down and down into the dog's saliva-filled mouth!

Ray Mellor (9)
Oldswinford CE Primary School, Oldswinford

Fierce And Frightened

There was a penguin made fun of for his croaky voice. He was a squeaky toy and he was left on the shelf. One day he met a dinosaur, the bravest of them all. He helped Penguin make a plan to escape, they called it 'the plan of the fierce and frightened'.
The day came. It was midnight; he waddled down the stairs and dinosaurs lifted him up to the letterbox. He jumped through and waddled to a toy maker. He fixed Penguin and gave him life, he was free.

Annabel Stark (9)

Oldswinford CE Primary School, Oldswinford

Teddy Falls Out Of Bed

The soldier, Tog came out of his sentry box and saw Teddy fall out of bed. He had to get Teddy back in bed. The doll tried to lift Teddy back but she could not do it.

Teddy sighed, "Will I ever get back in bed?"

He fell back and knocked over a box. Out of the box came some bricks. The bricks started to make stairs up to the bed! Teddy stood and climbed, carefully up the tall, towering stairs, to his snuggly home.

Jasper Bell (10)
Oldswinford CE Primary School, Oldswinford

The Money Box

The money box was on the shelf one day and he fell onto the floor. All the money came out. He came to life and picked it all back up. He found it hard work but in the end, he did it. He couldn't get back up so he tried and tried. He ended up making it... That's what happens when you try hard, you *will* make it!
The money box was super happy and over the moon!

Luke Parker (9)
Oldswinford CE Primary School, Oldswinford

Tinseltown Mysteries

Ronnie worked hard to finally solve this mystery, he couldn't believe he was about to discover the truth. The huge, steel door, covered in cobwebs, creaked as he entered the house. Mr Shortbottom stood at the dark fireplace, holding the beautiful spinning top with trembling hands. He dropped the spinning top. Suddenly, when Ronnie entered the room, the room exploded into dazzling, bright lights, like fireworks. In astonishment, Mr Shortbottom shouted, "I had to do this to save our town. I'm sorry." Ronnie knew things were about to get a lot worse for Tinseltown. Now he knew the whole, scary truth.

Maisy Webb (9)
Rushall Primary School, Rushall

Dash The Dinosaur

"It's my year!" exclaimed Dash. "I'm getting out of this toyshop." Suddenly, Dash saw his chance. He dived off the shelf and landed with a gentle thud, into an open bag. He buried himself deep, in hope that no one would spot him. Little did Dash know, there was a hole in the bottom of the bag! As the owner picked it up to leave, Dash's hopes crashed as he landed on the floor. He slowly looked up. A small boy reached towards him. The boy was wearing a T-shirt that said 'I love dinosaurs'. Dash's time was here.

Riley Binks
Rushall Primary School, Rushall

Teddy's Nightmare!

Zzzzz! Teddy opened one eye, cautiously. He realised he wasn't where he belonged... He was lying on the floor! All he could see were clothes and toys, scattered all over the thick, carpeted bedroom floor. He steadily got to his feet. "Ouch!" he shrieked as his soft paw trod on an abandoned Lego brick.

He tiptoed to the edge of the bed and climbed, with all his strength and might, back onto it from where he had fallen. He snuggled under his caring, best friend's arms. He was safe and warm again, exactly where he belonged.

Matthew Cheek (8)
Rushall Primary School, Rushall

Red Village

Once upon a time, lived two girls called Lino and Lisa. Lino was sick so Lisa went to get some magical berries in the dark forest. As Lisa was riding on her bike to get the magical berries for Lisa, a wolf jumped out of the bushes. It looked hungry and then Lisa saw the magical berries. Lisa saw some bunnies, so she used them as a distraction.

The big pack of wolves followed her home. She gave Lino the magical berries before she died. Lino saw a pack of wolves but she scared them all forever.

La'myah Pink (8)

Rushall Primary School, Rushall

The Crazy, Delicious Problem

Once upon a time, there lived two toys called Delicious Doughnut and Super Swirl. They both went on holiday together to Candy Land. In Candy Land, there were different kinds of candy! There was a chocolate rainbow fountain; a river full of treats and get ready for the best part... a candy house! While Delicious Doughnut and Super Swirl were having fun a crazy clown came chasing them. They screamed so loud and they ran back to Rainbow Land, where it was safe but Super Swirl kicked the crazy clown and everything was back to normal!

Keryane Fofana (10)

St Elizabeth's Catholic Primary School, Coventry

The Journey Back Home

Once upon a time, there was Bella, who lived with her mom and big sister. Bella had a favourite toy monkey she played with, called Max. Whenever Bella went to the play centre, she took Max along. It was time for Bella to go home but she forgot Max! When she got home the other toys saw that she didn't come back with Max and became worried!

They set off to find Max in the play centre. They climbed trees, jumped from houses and crossed roads to find Max before Bella found out. They found Max and went back home!

Kenechukwu Stephanie Osanebi (10)

St Elizabeth's Catholic Primary School, Coventry

The Final Escape

She was taken by a man. He carried her violently through dusty shelves, holding new and glossy toys. She glimmered without having to be cleaned. Her name was Star Shooter. She was the most beautiful of them all. She made lots of friends but her closest was Boots. Eager to find a new home, they performed a risky escape. It took them eight weeks to find themselves a new toyshop for a home. They journeyed on and it took a long time. They stopped at Toys 'R' Us. They were welcomed home!

Amber Ogblu (10)
St Elizabeth's Catholic Primary School, Coventry

Mr Strong

Mr Strong is the strongest toy in the whole wide world. He not only bends iron bars, he can tie them in knots and throw cannonballs as far as you or I could throw a tennis ball! The more eggs he eats, the stronger he gets.

One day, he saw a terrified farmer in a blazing fire.

"Help!" screamed the farmer.

"Is that your barn?" said Mr Strong.

"Yes!"

So he picked up the barn, went to a river and put it out.

Marcus Chand (9)

St Elizabeth's Catholic Primary School, Coventry

Help Me Someone

One breezy summer's day, Squashy, a little, cute toy, lived in West Liverpool, by the sea. He wanted to play out in the yucky mud. He took his glossy yellow wellies. Slowly but suddenly, he started to sink as he was brainwashed by the beautiful dolphins, swimming. Before he noticed, he was halfway down! There was nowhere to ask for help, except the sardine seller, who was miles away. A massive whale leapt out and saved Squashy!

Kaisa Briella Mfasoni (10)
St Elizabeth's Catholic Primary School, Coventry

The Monkey

Once upon a time, there lived a toy monkey whose name was Emily. The monkey was so good so she went to play with her friends.

The next day she went out and started to be a bit naughty. She bit her friends and was saying mean things.

On Saturday, she didn't see any more friends and she didn't know why, so she went outside and knocked on their doors but nobody answered except for her cousins.

Shreya Sahota (9)

St Elizabeth's Catholic Primary School, Coventry

Talking Toys

One night, a toy horse started talking in a little girl's bedroom. She said to Mermaid, "Will you play with me, Mermaid?"
Mermaid said, "Not now, I want to go to sleep!"
Horse said, "Will you play with me, Unicorn?"
Unicorn said, "No, my rainbow tail will get dirty."
"All I want is to play with you!" Horse shouted.
"I think that woke our owner," said Mermaid.
The little girl said, "I won't hurt you!"
"Okay, let's be friends," said Horse.
"You must promise never to tell anyone about us," said Unicorn.
"Okay, I promise."

Isabella Bird (7)
St Joseph's Catholic Primary School, Sutton Coldfield

Teddy's Big Day

"Teddy, breakfast!" Momma Teddy said.
"Coming!" said Teddy. "Today I'm wearing my
sparkly T-shirt and my skinny jeans."
"You look nice, Teddy."
"Thanks, can we go to the park?"
"Yes we can, Teddy. Have your breakfast, then we
can start walking."
Teddy really liked breakfast. "Let's go to the park!"
Teddy scooted off.
At the park they saw their friends. It looked like
they'd lost something but Teddy found what they
were looking for. It was a keyring. "Thanks Teddy!
You're a hero!" Then they all played in the
playground.

Poppy Parnham (7)
St Joseph's Catholic Primary School, Sutton Coldfield

The Adventure Bear

One golden, bright morning, a bear got left out from all the other bears.
One day, he set off into the misty outdoors. Firstly, he met noisy monkeys and said, "Will you be my friend?" but they ignored him. "Will anyone be my best friend?" he mumbled.
Then, one day, he found a little cottage. *Oh, how pretty!* he thought to himself. He didn't know a little girl lived in there.
When he opened the door, it didn't make a noise. "Winnie," she called, as he woke up, "are you still asleep?"
"Yes." It was just a dream.

Lydia Eustace (8)
St Joseph's Catholic Primary School, Sutton Coldfield

The Room Roamer

Why am I so untidy? Just look at me! My room is a horrid mess. I need help. Feeling tired, I fall asleep. A buzzing sound wakes me. Red lights flash and I notice my toy robot. He whispers, "I have sensors, they detect untidiness. I can help you."
I scramble onto the carpet, as the roaming robot starts his work, firstly pairing up socks and putting them in drawers. Next, he hangs up my favourite dress, which has been lost for ages.
Within minutes, my room is immaculate, I give the robot a huge hug. "You're amazing, toy robot!"

Freya James (7)
St Joseph's Catholic Primary School, Sutton Coldfield

O' Fair Cloud Of Delightness

Once, there was a dull world called Glum Cloud. Crystal Cloudy didn't have any friends, so he had to live a lonely life. Crystal looked smart and always followed the best choices.

One day, he was sent to a new home. It was exciting to have a new mother but only the children turned out to be kind. Their names were Benjamin and Leila. When they first saw Crystal, it was strange because they were dragons. As they grew, their stepmother died but the three of them still stayed as a family. Surprisingly Leila had two children, Belle and Oli.

Anabel Katrina Eve Collins (8)

St Joseph's Catholic Primary School, Sutton Coldfield

Sleepover

Isa and her sister were going to their friend's doll sleepover. They had to pack up pillows, clothes, toothbrushes, toothpaste, make-up, books and pyjamas. When they arrived, Bella's mum prepared spa items, for example; a hot tub, body scrub, body masks, massage oil, cream, towels and juice. After the amazing spa, they had a make-up programme. They learned how to use make-up items such as eyebrow pencils, eyeliner, eyeshadow, glitter, lip liner, blusher and foundation. They slept in bunkbeds with the humans!

Yien Gao (7)
St Joseph's Catholic Primary School, Sutton Coldfield

The Hatchimals' Great Idea

"I'm bored!" moaned Pinkchipadee.
"We'll find something," explained BlueRaspoon.
Then Cloudraggle had an idea! "We'll
fly!" whispered Cloudraggle excitedly. Every
Hatchimal had a big smile on their face. Every
Hatchimal's favourite thing to do was fly.
Suddenly, the Hatchimals started panicking
because Olivia woke up. "Who are you?" said
Olivia, with a really puzzled face. "Wait, you're my
cute Hatchimals," said Olivia, realising very quickly.
Olivia always dreamed of her toys coming to life.
"Will I see you tomorrow?" said Olivia politely.
"You will if you're good and go to bed on time,"
said BlueRaspoon with a big, big smile.

Olivia Hayes (8)
St Mary's Catholic Primary School, Wolverhampton

Magical Evening

On the night before Christmas morning, the children swished into their beds, in the neighbourhood of London. "Ho, ho, ho!" Mister Claus merrily called out to the snowy city. Zooming down the airy chimney, the present of a little boy's dream sprung right under the jubilant, festive tree. *Burst!* goes the leaping gift box, as a plastic dinosaur shot out like a rocket! Later on, it chomped through the pink tree's leaves and devoured and guzzled down the family's chocolate pie - what a dramatic night! Racing noisily around the room, the dinosaur flew and... "What happened?" boomed the exhausted children.

Carlotta Susanna Cruzada (11)

St Mary's Catholic Primary School, Wolverhampton

A Siberian Gift

Alisa and her favourite toy wolf, Major were darting to the shop to purchase everything needed for Christmas that year. Without her knowing, Major smoothly slid out of her backpack, through the window and into freezing, deep, hard, Siberian snow. Major gained life! Suddenly an enormous falcon scooped him up into the clouds. Major struggled, cluelessly, without an escape...
Flying through the North Pole's harsh weather, the falcon's grip loosened, leading Major to land on Santa's toy-wrapping factory. Major stuck Alisa's address onto his fur, hopped into Santa's bag and arrived at Alisa's just in time for Christmas!

Aash Merin Mathew (10)
St Mary's Catholic Primary School, Wolverhampton

Humans Vs Teddy Bears

"Sergeant, I've scanned the area. Coast is clear!" whispered Teddy Bear 3.

"Teddy bears, it's time to go. Be careful!" With the enemy in their beds, the mischievous creatures jumped over the humans and dashed to make their escape.

Lining up on the rough carpet, there was one thing the teddy bears had to do; plan revenge. "Teddy bears, get ready for battle!" screamed Teddy Bear 2.

"Incoming!" shouted one bear!

A scary-shaped figure came bounding in but actually, it was the dog. He squished all the bears and started licking them. "Uhh! Disgusting!" they shouted.

Zenia Dillon (10)

St Mary's Catholic Primary School, Wolverhampton

The Hazardous Trap!

"Argh!" shouted the bear, loudly. "Where am I?" he asked.
In the darkness, with no light, the bear was staying alone. He was very confused. "I don't understand!" he continued. "Wait!" There was a sound. "What was that?" Two red eyes appeared, one massive mouth and even some spiky teeth. "Don't tell me it's a monster! Hello, who is there?" questioned the bear. But there wasn't any reply. So he got angry. "Help!" he screamed.
Where was the bear? Who took him? When will he return? What is with him? These questions can't be answered.

Maria Burlacu (9)
St Mary's Catholic Primary School, Wolverhampton

Brave Sir Miaows A Lot

A day after Dennis had gone to a new school, when he got home, he went upstairs. All the toys were moving. "Argh!" shouted Dennis.
As he went back downstairs Sir Miaows A Lot told every toy, "Calm down, what if we made him our friend?"
The toys actually liked the idea. So Sir Miaows A Lot calmed down too. He ran downstairs and tried to find Dennis but he could not see him anywhere. Then, Dennis came and screamed again. "Argh!"
Sir Miaows A Lot whispered, "Let's be best friends, Dennis."
"Okay," answered Dennis.

Petru-Rares Alin Ignatescu (9)

St Mary's Catholic Primary School, Wolverhampton

Fuzzy In The Forest...

"Oh, where could she be?" asked Layla. Her toy, Fuzzy the unicorn, was lost in the garden! How lonely she was!
"I'm so scared!" Fuzzy cried. Terrified she hopped through the garden.
To Fuzzy, the grass was a forest. Suddenly, out of the grass emerged a beetle. Not big for us, but huge for Fuzzy! She didn't need telling twice, for she was already off! Soon after, she could barely breathe! Fortunately, Layla, now crying, just happened to be passing by. "Fuzzy!" she screamed, picking up Fuzzy very gently. Now, Laya always keeps Fuzzy with her.

Laura Skurpel (10)
St Mary's Catholic Primary School, Wolverhampton

The Night-Time Mystery

As Lexie sleeps Teddy comes alive. "Ouch!" screeched the teddy, as it stood up. "Let's get off this bed!" As soon as he was off the bed Teddy, who was very curious, looked around the room for the music players and some CDs. He started to play music and had a massive party, including lots of toys! Lexie's room had turned into a whopping, glorious, crazy party. When the teddy noticed the time, he told everyone anxiously to go back to their hiding spots and boxes. As soon as possible, everyone was back in bed.

"What's happened?" Lexie groaned.

Holly Mary Janet Conlan (10)

St Mary's Catholic Primary School, Wolverhampton

The Quest For The Younger One

Michelle was sleeping one night when she heard a noise. She woke up and trembled while taking a glimpse of the door. "Is that you, Mom?"
"No, darling."
Michelle looked under her bed. It was her teddy! She got off her bed and the teddy climbed from underneath. She had the urge to hold his hand, so she did. She was transported to a weird land.
"We're going to find my brother!" said Teddy.
They traipsed through snow and mud. Finally, they reached the cave and rescued the younger teddy. Michelle awoke. It was all a dream... or was it?

Scarlet Grace Winters (10)
St Mary's Catholic Primary School, Wolverhampton

The Magical Unicorn

Molly ran as fast as she could. The rain was pouring down, she and her fluffy unicorn were soaked. Suddenly she tripped and her unicorn dropped from her hand, into a big puddle. Molly looked back and couldn't believe her eyes; Unicorn was no longer a fluffy toy, she was a fully grown, real unicorn! She said, "Jump on my back, I will take you home to safety!"

Molly picked herself up from the wet and muddy ground and got on the unicorn's back. "Let's fly you home!" Unicorn shouted. Molly hugged her tight and they flew through the rain!

Lacie-Lei Thompson (9)

St Mary's Catholic Primary School, Wolverhampton

Lucky Timmy

Whilst I was at school, Timmy, my soft toy bear, sneaked outside, climbed up the tree nearby and sat on a branch. He probably wanted to find a better place to stay. Suddenly a stork perched near him. Politely, Timmy requested that the bird take him to the biggest toyshop. Surprisingly, the stork agreed! At the shop, Timmy looked around. The toys seemed lonely. No home or best friend for them. Timmy realised how Elijah snuggled and loved him all these years. They flew back home. As he thanked the stork, he exclaimed, "I'm lucky, I'm going to stay!"

Elijah Majaducon (9)
St Mary's Catholic Primary School, Wolverhampton

Toys Alone

It was windy and a stormy night when I left my toys alone but I forgot to lock the door. A man came into my room and started breaking my toys. Smashing their heads on the floor and stamping on them. One toy had the idea to get revenge. His name was Tevin. He started setting traps, so next time the man would be trapped.

Next Tuesday I travelled to the shop. I locked the door and somehow he got in but the traps were activated. The neighbours were complaining that there was screaming.

Tadiwa Chikomo (9)

St Mary's Catholic Primary School, Wolverhampton

The Lost Teddy

Topsy was upset. She had lost her most favourite toy in the world, Tommy Teddy. Everyone had looked everywhere for her but no one could find her.

As time went on Topsy grew more and more upset. The next morning she was even sadder and headed into the front room for her breakfast. But, as she did this, she got a big surprise. Sitting on the chair was her teddy, all snuggled up in a blanket. He didn't need anyone to find him, he was clever enough to find his own way home!

Abbie McManus (10)

St Mary's Catholic Primary School, Wolverhampton

Extraordinary Escape

It was six in the morning and there was one Berny Bear and six Dilly Dolls, sat on a white, metal shelf, sneakily Berny fell off the shelf and snuck out of his colourful Berny box. However, Berny struggled to help six Dilly Dolls out. When all the dolls were out, they snuck out of the shop, crossed the busy road and snuck into a little girl's room, who had always wanted a Berny Bear and Dilly Dolls!
In the morning the workmen didn't mind because they had a new stock.

Keira Swatman (9)
St Mary's Catholic Primary School, Wolverhampton

Bella And Her Adventures

Bella was a teddy bear who comes alive at night. Bella's friends also come alive during the night. One time, her owner had bought a full set of toys to play with when she was awake. Not knowing that they did this, Bella wanted to bond with the newbies. As she drew closer and closer, somehow, she started to be hypnotised. The next thing she knew, she'd arrived in the North Pole! Just going with the flow, she wandered around happily and joyfully, loving her life!

Lucy May Nicholas (11)
St Mary's Catholic Primary School, Wolverhampton

The Big Little T-Rex

Once upon a time, little toy men went on an adventure. They travelled through a portal, to the jungle! They walked and walked and at last, they reached an amazing place. It was full of dinosaurs! There was a velociraptor and a stegosaurus and suddenly, they saw a T-rex. It chased them. Eventually, they reached a big cave and ran inside. They saw a place to hide. They quickly ran there and they hid.

Cian William Walker (8)

St Mary's Catholic Primary School, Wolverhampton

My Magic Jack-In-The-Box

Once, lived a girl, named Mary. It was her birthday and her mum and dad bought a jack-in-the-box. However, she didn't like it, so she broke it. Suddenly a twinkle sparkled and she saw herself in an unknown land, unexpectedly she heard footsteps. Two fellows came and asked if she needed help. She had to go home, she had the pieces of the jack-in-the-box. Finally, she could go home!

Favour Erhabor (10)
St Mary's Catholic Primary School, Wolverhampton

Untitled

"Hey," whispered a mysterious voice, as a small, dragon-like creature crawled across the bedroom floor.
"Stop, you're going to get caught!"
exclaimed another voice but more feminine...
Suddenly a large shadow leapt over the creature. A huge, hammer-like object (a foot) crushed the poor thing, you could hear everyone gasp as the remains scattered around the room. "I told him not to because I knew Master was coming!" said a Barbie doll.
"We better hide before he comes," quickly spoke another voice.
"Okay," answered the head of the creature. All the toys fell into a quiet, soundless sleep.

Anveer Gill (9)
Woodfield Junior School, Penn

Midnight Mischief

On Friday at 9.30pm, Mr Rhys closed the shutter, began walking home, not knowing what mischief would take place in his absence. The dolls started gossiping, the soldiers started marching, the babies started crying. All of a sudden, from underneath the toy box, came Darth Vader and his army of Stormtroopers. Action Man, James Bond and G.I. Joe all sprung into action. The evildoer and his army of tyrants were no match for the heroes.

The shutter started to open. "I knew I was forgetting something," said Mr Rhys, looking for his phone, everything was exactly where he'd left it.

Anshpreet Kaur (9)
Woodfield Junior School, Penn

Magical Dolls

At night, the dolls came to life, Snow White had an apple and found herself in Mexico, where she found Belle. "Hi, Snow!" said Belle. They began to talk.

The next day came. "Hey Snow, I have something to show you."

They went into a sparkly forest. "Please come home, Belle," said Snow.

"No," said Belle.

A week went by, then Belle came. "I'm staying because I miss you," said Belle, softly.

They became known as the magical dolls and Snow learned that you don't have to act like a princess, you just have to believe you are one.

Simran Bansal (9)
Woodfield Junior School, Penn

The Day Gillian Met A Unicorn

3,000 years after the evil unicorn's disappearance Gillian set off to find her friend. Gillian walked to the unicorn castle and heard a twinkle. The tall, shiny castle arose before her. *Bang!* Gillian knocked on the door. It opened. Isabella stood in front of her. "Gillian, it's been so long, I've got bad news!"

Hours later the sky turned black and the evil unicorn arrived. Gillian was told about two of her friends, Chelsea and Lini, who were going to change. He came and turned them into their normal selves. Lini and Chelsea were Gillian's pets, forever.

Chloe Jayne Padley-Whiles (9)
Woodfield Junior School, Penn

To The Rescue

Deep down in Hamley's storeroom, Coco the dog was yelping and barking for help. He had got stuck in a box and couldn't get out. It was Christmas Eve and all the toys were saying, "What's that dreadful sound?"

"It sounds like someone is in desperate need of help!"

"Well, it is up to us to find out!"

They all followed the noise, they got so close that they didn't even notice Coco was behind them. They turned around, lifted the flap of the box and there was Coco... Now Christmas would be the best one they'd ever had.

Gurpej Singh (9)

Woodfield Junior School, Penn

Toy Town

"Who's there?" said James, the security guard.
"Me," said a small distant voice.
James turned around and looked at the back of the toyshop. It was closed, so nobody else should have been there. Further and further in he went until he made a sudden stop. He realised the toys in the toyshop weren't ordinary toys. He was in for a whole lot more than he expected...

Vinaya Rai (9)
Woodfield Junior School, Penn

YoungWriters

Est.1991

YOUNG WRITERS
INFORMATION

We hope you have enjoyed reading this book – and that you will continue to in the coming years.

If you're a young writer who enjoys reading and creative writing, or the parent of an enthusiastic poet or story writer, do visit our website **www.youngwriters.co.uk**. Here you will find free competitions, workshops and games, as well as recommended reads, a poetry glossary and our blog.

If you would like to order further copies of this book, or any of our other titles, then please give us a call or visit **www.youngwriters.co.uk**.

Young Writers
Remus House
Coltsfoot Drive
Peterborough
PE2 9BF
(01733) 890066 / 898110
info@youngwriters.co.uk

 @YoungWritersUK    @YoungWritersCW